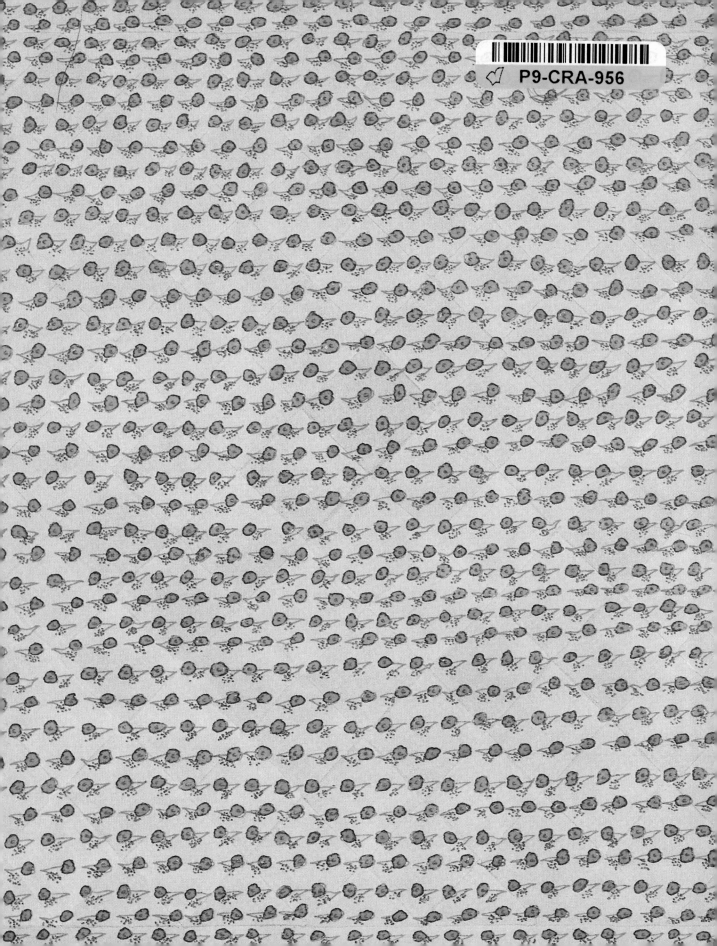

P9-CRA-956

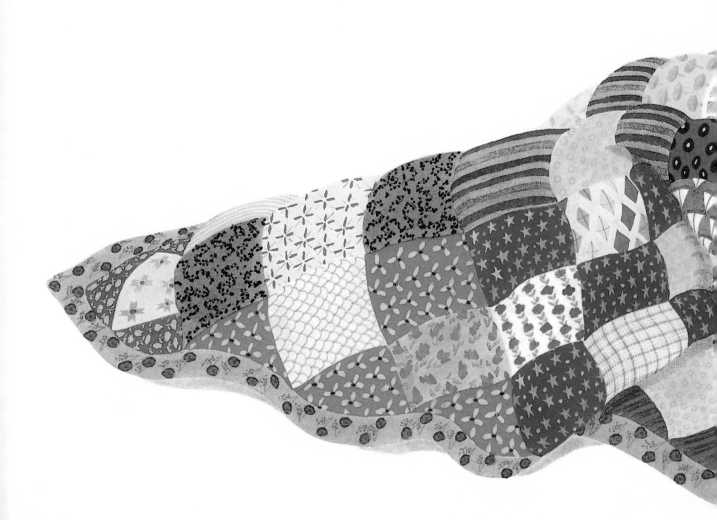

# The Quilt
## Ann Jonas

**For Nina**

As a part of the HBJ TREASURY OF LITERATURE, 1993 Edition, this edition is published by special arrangement with Greenwillow Books, a division of William Morrow, Publishers, Inc.

Grateful acknowledgment is made to Greenwillow Books, a division of William Morrow & Company, Inc. for permission to reprint *The Quilt* by Ann Jonas. Copyright © 1984 by Ann Jonas.

Printed in the United States of America

ISBN 0-15-300316-2

2 3 4 5 6 7 8 9 10    059    96    95    94    93

**HBJ** Harcourt Brace Jovanovich, Inc.
Orlando Austin San Diego Chicago Dallas New York

I have a new quilt.

It's to go on my
new grown-up bed.

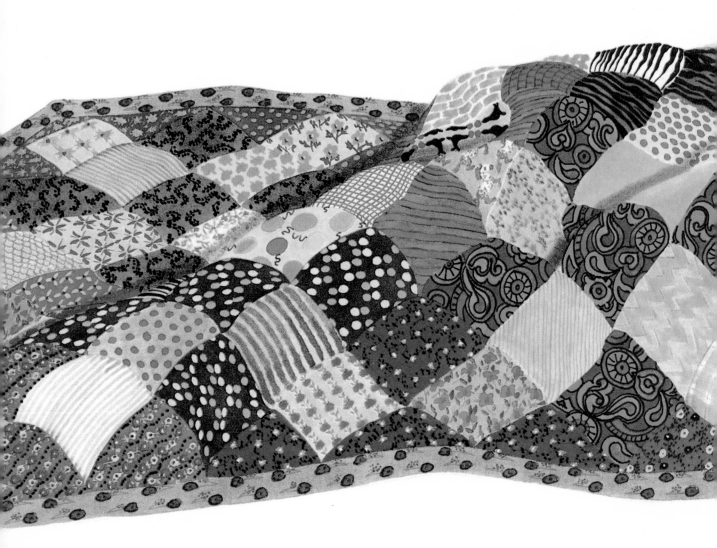

My mother and father
made it for me. They used
some of my old things.
Here are my first curtains
and my crib sheet. Sally
is lying on my baby pajamas.

That's the shirt I wore on my second birthday.
This piece is from my favorite pants. They got too small. The cloth my mother used to make Sally is here somewhere.
I can't find it now.

I know I won't be able
to go to sleep tonight.

It almost looks
like a little town....

I can't find Sally!

She wouldn't like it here.
Sally!

What if someone took her home? Sally!

If she hid here,
I'd never find her.
Sally!

I see her!

**Good morning, Sally.**

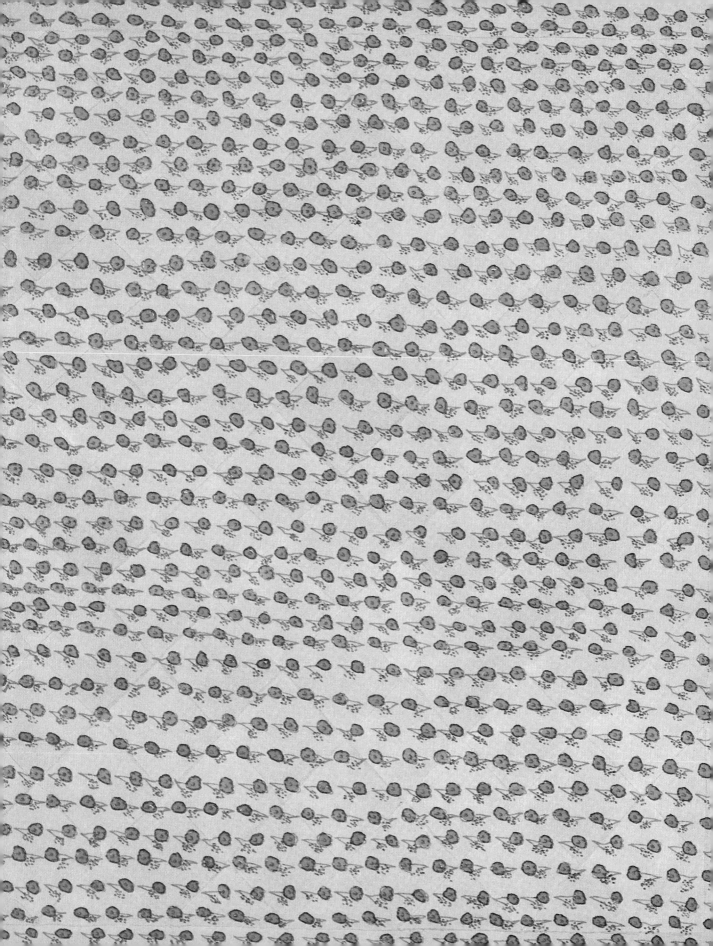